A note to parents

Although we've used the expressions "Number One" and "Number Two" in our book, you may wish to substitute whatever expressions are used in your own home for these two functions.

Whatever the words, we should try to remember that in all times, and in all places, children have put up some resistance to being toilet trained: it seems to be part of growing up. Punishing the child does little more than create bad feelings in both child and parent about an already sensitive subject, and rarely speeds up the process. A little patience (and a lot of love) are much more helpful in this important rite of passage. We hope this book will help as well.

Library of Congress Cataloging-in-Publication Data
Potty time.
   p. cm.
  "A Little Simon book."
  Summary: Two-year-old Milly has a few discouraging accidents in the course of learning how to use her potty, but she eventually masters the process.
  ISBN 0-671-65896-4
  [1. Toilet training – Fiction.]
PZ7.P859 1988
[E] – dc 19

ISBN: 0-671-65896-4

87-21910
CIP
AC

POTTY TIME

Illustrated by
Jonathan Langley

Written by
Anne Civardi

Little Simon
Published by Simon & Schuster, Inc. New York

Millie Marsh is nearly two. Her big sister, Candy, is five and her brother, Chester, is still a baby.

Millie can walk and run and talk a little. She likes to play with her toys.

Millie still wears diapers all the time, but soon she will learn to sit on the potty.

4

Candy doesn't wear diapers. She sits on the toilet
when she wants to make Number One or Number Two.

One day, Millie's mom gives her a red potty.
Millie shows it to her best friend, Polly.

Polly has a potty of her own. "You make Number One and Number Two in it," she says to Millie.

Today, Millie wants to sit on her new potty. Mom
takes off Millie's diaper and sits down beside her.

8

Millie sits and sits and sits, and tries hard to go.
But when she gets up, her potty is empty.

The next day is very hot. Millie takes off her clothes to play in the garden.

She makes a puddle on the ground. "Never mind,"
says Dad. "But please use the potty next time."

One day, Millie needs her potty badly. She runs to her bedroom as fast as she can.

She sits on the potty and makes a big Number Two.
"Look at what I've done," Millie says proudly.

Now Millie doesn't want to wear diapers anymore.
Mom gives her some special pants to put on.

Millie thinks her pants are much better than diapers.
She shows them to Candy and Chester.

But one day when Millie is very busy, she makes a puddle on the kitchen floor.

16

"It was just an accident," says Mom. She isn't angry
and Millie helps clean up the mess.

Later Mom and Dad take Millie on a picnic. She drinks a lot of juice and wants to make Number One badly.

18

Dad takes her behind a big bush. Millie thinks that it is fun to make Number One outside.

Now Millie uses her potty all the time. She takes it with her nearly everywhere she goes.

Sometimes, she even sits on the toilet like Candy.
She hardly ever wets her pants anymore.

Soon Millie uses the toilet instead of her red potty.
She is a big girl now.

22

Sometimes Mom helps her a little. When Millie gets
off the toilet, she washes her hands.

Chester still wears diapers all the time. But Millie is teaching him to sit on the potty.

24